THE PERFECTLY IMPERFECT CHICKEN

By Rick Rieser

Illustrated by Daniel Seward

Percy The Perfectly Imperfect Chicken
By Rick Rieser
Illustrated by Daniel Seward

ISBN 9 781607 469995

Published by:
FastPencil, Inc.
3131 Bascom Ave. Suite 150
Campbell, CA 95008
www.FastPencil.com

To all the people I promised I would dedicate this book, especially my beautiful daughter Gracie.

It was quiet in the henhouse,
And just one o'clock.
CRACK hatched an egg,
One more in the flock.

All the chickens were joyful,
"One more in our pen!"
"What shall we name him?"
"Percy" said proud Mama Hen.

The chickens peered at Percy,
And inspected real close …
To make sure he was perfect,
From his beak to his toes.

"We chickens are perfect,"
Said three older hens,
Then started a chant ,
Learned way back when:

"Our feathers are white,
From our combs to the ground,
Except for our wings,
They are speckled with brown.

Our wings are short,
As everyone knows.

Each beak must be yellow,

Each foot has three toes."

Staring at Percy,
They fluttered around,
Inspecting his comb,
And feathery down.

Three toes on each foot,
"That's a yes," they did say.
His beak perfect yellow,
They shouted, "Hurray!"

As they looked closer,
At his down feathered wing,
Brought out the spy glass,
And noticed ... something.

"Look at those speckles,"
All of them said.
"They are not brown,
In fact, they are red!"

"Please leave him alone!"
Percy's mom stated strong.
"Let him grow up,
And now, move along.

For he was just born,
His feathers are new,
I've heard of a notion,
I believe that is true.

As chicks get older,
Their feathers can change,
And turn different colors,
Even though that sounds strange."

"That better be true,"
Those old hens quickly said,
"Our short wings are perfect,
Brown-speckled, not red."

"Mama, what's perfect?"
Asked Percy with fear.
She waited to tell him,
Til no one was near.

See, Mama was sorry,
Percy so closely was checked.
For any chicken not perfect,
Would surely be pecked!

"Don't worry," said Mama,
"I'll hide you away.
Your wings will turn brown,
We'll wait for that day."

In the days that followed,
They did all that they could.
Percy hid in the grass,

And he hid in the woods.

Percy got bigger,
By each hour and day.
Percy was changing,
But not the right way.

For he grew tall,
With a shine on his beak,
And a beautiful comb,
With three toes on his feet.

But his feathers, OH MY!
They were not white and brown,
But red and bright colors,
From his comb to the ground.

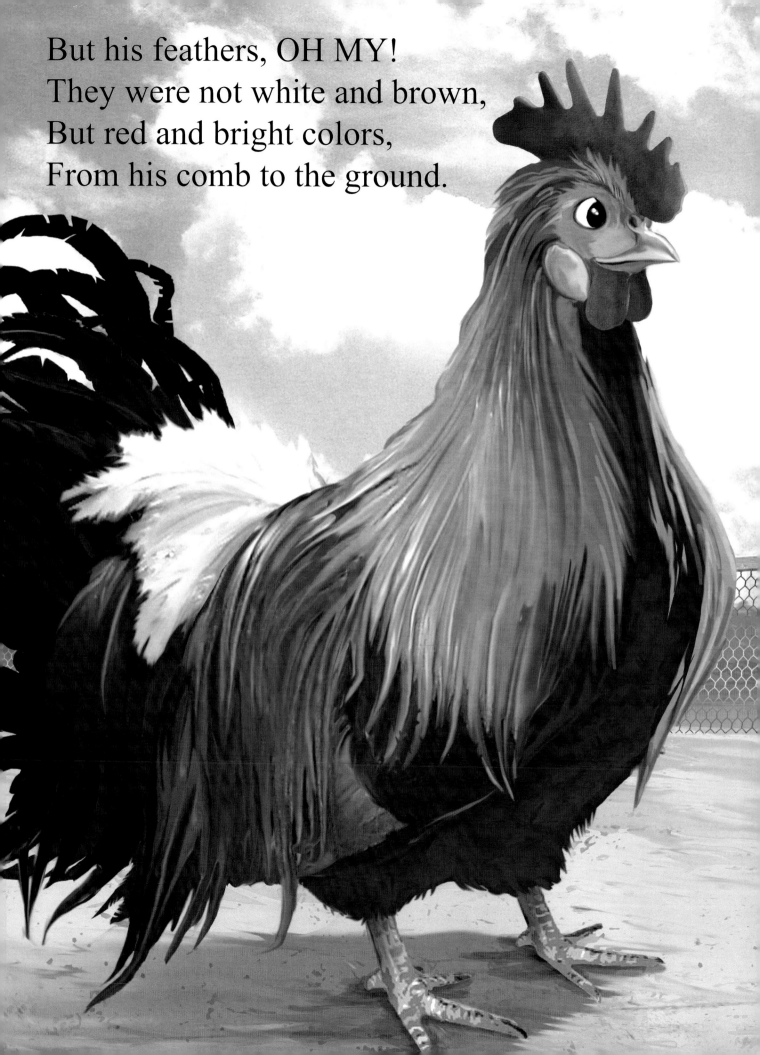

When those old hens saw this,
They started to faint.
"Percy's not perfect,
He looks colored with paint!"

Then they looked closer.
"Something else too is wrong!
Look at his wings ...
Not short, they are long!"

They all gathered and clucked,
Away from his ears.
They talked about pecking,
He grew sad with a tear.

Those old hens came forward,
 Then Percy could hear,
"You are not perfect,
 Your pecking is near."

Percy grew fearful,
Flapped his wings and asked, "Why?"
He kept flapping and flapping,
Til he started to …

FLY!

He flew high in the air,
And circled the pen.
He flew higher and higher,
Away from those hens.

Those chickens were mad,
As they scratched at the sand.

Yet from the sky they were different.
Then his feet touched the land.

In his heart was wisdom
As he stood on the ground
Percy knew what to do
As those hens gathered round.

He approached them directly,
No longer did care.
Spoke to them clearly,
"I saw you up there."

He walked to the first hen,
Right up to her cheek,
And asked her real softly,
"A spot on your beak?"

Less soft to the second,
"You think nobody knows.
Please show your left foot,
And all four of your toes."

The third hen moved backward,
Away from his words.
She wanted to run fast,
Away from those birds.

"When you were squawking and flapping,
I most clearly could see,
Those feathers you hide,
All red…just like me."

All three of those hens,
Stopped chanting their song,
And forever stopped pecking,
For they knew it was wrong.

Something changed in the henhouse that day--
A new way of thinking that won't go away.

"Mama what's perfect?"
Percy still did persist.
Mama said, "Percy, it's nothing.
It doesn't exist."

About the Author: **Rick Rieser**

Percy the Perfectly Imperfect Chicken represents the culmination of the author's 25 year career as a writer, nationally recognized children's advocate and most importantly, chicken farmer. He has developed resources for children of all ages that emphasize and focus on the inner strength and potential that exists in every child.

He is a cum laude graduate of Capital Law School, earned two degrees from The Ohio State University including a Masters in Family Science. He has received numerous awards including the Martin Luther King Jr Award (Ohio), 1997 Friend of Education Award, the Peacemaker Award and other national recognitions for his work. Rick resides in Orient, Ohio near Columbus with his eight year old daughter Gracie, four rabbits (and counting), numerous rare chickens including Percy the Perfectly Imperfect Chicken!

About the Illustrator: **Daniel Seward**

Dan Seward discovered he was an artist in the third grade while living with his parents in North Idaho and has since been using art to serve primarily other artists in schools and communities in Northern California. Dan loves the wonder-full mix of art and young people and how the imagination can spark the creative process in anyone who is open to it.